POWWOW!

Catherine Mangieri

Rosen Classroom Books & Materials™
New York

We are going to the powwow!
I like going to the powwow.
It is fun!

People wear special clothes at the powwow.

People play drums at the powwow.

Men dance at the powwow.

Women dance at the powwow.

Children dance at the powwow, too.

People sing songs at the powwow.

People ride horses at the powwow.

People see friends at the powwow.

People eat bread at the powwow.
We eat, too!

The powwow is fun, but it is time to go home now.